SO-BFB-402

A MUPPET™ PICTURE READER

Fozzie's Bubble Bath

Written by Stuart Bergen
Illustrated by Rick Brown

©2005 Jim Henson Productions, Inc. All rights reserved. No part of this book may be reproduced or copied in any form without written permission from the copyright owner. MUPPET PRESS, MUPPETS, and character names and likenesses are trademarks of Jim Henson Productions, Inc. ISBN: 1-59226-210-4. Printed in China.

Published by Big Tent Entertainment, 216 West 18th Street, New York, New York, 10011.

Ding-dong.

The – rang.

"Who is it?" asked.

"It is .

I am blue."

" , do you mean

you are sad?" said.

 opened the .

"No," said.

"I am really blue."

 held up a

and .

"I just painted my ."

"You need a bath,"

 told .

"If you say so,"

 said.

 went into

's .

He went up the .

He found the .

6

"See you later, ,"

 told .

Then he closed

the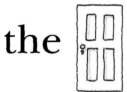

and filled the .

"Oh, ," called .

"Where is the ?"

"The  is on

the ,"

 said.

"Thanks," said.

 got in the .

He made lots of .

"Oh, ," called .

"Where is your rubber ?"

"My rubber is on the ," said.

 put the

in the  .

"  baths are fun!"

 said.

At last, was done.

"Oh, ," called .

"Now I need a ."

"A is on the ,"  said.

"Thanks,"  said.

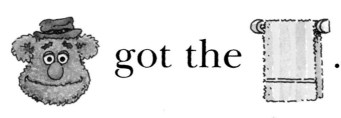 got the .

He dried his

and his ![foot]

and everything

in between.

 opened the .

"Thanks,  ,"

said .

"That was fun.

And I am not

blue anymore."

But everything else was!

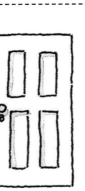

Kermit	bell
door	Fozzie
paint	brush
house	wagon

bathtub	stairs
soap	alligator
bubbles	sink
shelf	duck

nose	towel
fish	toes
car	boat
book	tree